"WATASHI WA"

私は

ISBN: 9780692725764

VAL MAKOTO.

私は

WRITTEN BY:

VAL MAKOTO

"著: ヴァル誠"

INNER GUIDE

"インナーガイド"

私は

"GOOD MORNING"

"TRAVEL TREASURES"

"DÉJÀ VU"

私は

"THIS."

"MOVIE WOO"

"WHAT DOES YOUR HEART SAY?"

私は

それです。
"THAT'S IT."
☺

"GOOD MORNING"

おはようございます

ONCE AGAIN, SOOTHINGLY, MY ORGANICALLY REDOUBLED DARK MATTER AWAKENS ME AT SUNRISE.

IN EFFECT, I CONSCIOUSLY LAZE IN MY BED, AND SIGHTLESSLY GAWK AT THE SATISFACTORY VOLUME OF MY STUDIO APARTMENT...

I listen closely to the room's silence.

And the room's silence, reciprocating my observance, attentively glares at my senses.

私は

Delicately regulating my
breathing, carelessly minding
a bourgeoning, inward-
centered brightness, I listen
closer.

Hence, I feel and hear my
heart palpitating; apace with
its support to my additional,
fully-functional, fully-
intact, bodily fixings.

I yearns to intensify
introspection, and listen
closer, but, *I knows* that if
I does so, I is bound to
undoubtedly evoke weighty
indolence in *me*.

Contentedly evading my
reflection, for now, I lift
my head towards the ceiling,
and joyously saunter to my
curtained window.

I analyze my illustrious megalopolis's, currently overcast, eastern skyline.

And ordinarily, while wholly realizing that there is an unquestionable possibility that precipitation will soon drizzle on my western slice of the highest, habitable tier of the inner-city's eldest unit of square-stack apartments, I grow further ecstatic.

I like breakfast; but I do not *love* breakfast. So, withdrawing my attentions from the natural happenings that are wonderfully happening outside my window, I redirect my ~~time~~ and vigour to café-runner delivered ice-coffee ingestion, defecation, bathing, nude facial hair shaving, nude milk supping, nude deft mechanistic tinkering, and nude periodic urination.

Musing on my cyclic plans of
solar noon reconditioned junk
selling in the trading post
district, I nakedly re-inset
twelve refurbished
commodities in to my wee
endearing hoard-bot, Kalifia,
and nakedly command her to
scoot to, and adjoin with,
the hull of my vehicle.

Subsequently, I embellish my
naked, universally appealing,
light copper-skinned body
with grey ankle socks, and,
scrotum-pally, grey boxer
briefs; and carefully don a
gold choker, a hazelnut 'I
Love Boobies' graffitied
long-sleeved tee-shirt, khaki
cargo trousers, and a duo of
waterproofed casual boots
that happen to be soot-black.

Preparing to reunite myself with the populace, I nimbly nab my pastel-green hooded jacket from my coat rack and start to scour its many pockets for my identification wristband.

Following a minimal search, I regain, from my jacket's right breastbone pocket, my wrist-worn passport to a luxurious human lifetime.

I cannot pilot modern modes of transportation, maintain currency, tangible or intangible, nor value *ideal citizen* incentives, intangible or tangible, to mention meagre disadvantages non-improvising-individuums have, without *live*, terra alliance-issued, identification wristwear.

Alongside a mighty, lone strike of thunder, I extend my left pointer-finger outward, and swipe it through the 'OPEN DOOR' icon on my front door's control panel; and, in result of my intently concentrated energies, the door scales instantaneously.

I exit my urbanus room,
gleefully humming a
fashionable tune, and stand
in the median of the
sidewalk, and briefly scan
Kali's ongoing linkage to the
starboard flank of my
parallel-docked transport,
the Little Kahuna.

Bestowing an end to my gay
humming, I silently loiter in
gratefulness; marveling at
the Little Kahuna's salmon-
tinted canopy, two-passenger
salmon leather and wood-
upholstered cockpit, and,
flawless, salmon-zigzagged,
verde hull.

I laugh at how empty I feel.

I gaze to my left, and I gaze to my right; I see no one at either angle.

Upbeat and surely, by speaking assertively in to my identification wristband, I transmit input to my vessel.

I:

"Start Kahuna!"

My transport obediently activates; its canopy sweeps, skyward...

A BREATHY, HIGH AND SOFT VOICE:
"Where are *you* hauling off
to, *mister sexy*?"

I punctually turn myself
around to review the locale
in which the voice came from,
thinking that I am
confronting a hallucination,
and I become aware of the
prettiest, made-up kitten
that I have ever seen.

As I onset to salivate at the
idea of *dominating* this
splendidly presented teenaged
female, who has placed
herself in to the
guardianship of a ruby red
hands-free umbrella, a lone
raindrop strikes my curly,
brunette-ish pompadour.

Accordingly, I establish the
use of my jacket's hood.

And the rain begins to
lightly pour, aslant.

The kitten, possessing
assistance from sensuous,
crimson closed-toed high-heel
shoes, stands tall afore mine
intelligent sensitivities,
slim built and pale-skinned,
posing, and snickering,
marketing plump, jiggly and
freckled buttocks, and
teasingly, repetitively,
flashing enormous, freckled
breasts, which are scantily
hidden by a crimson
miniskirt, and partway bared
by a moderately unzipped,
crimson quilted coat.

The kitten forcibly grapples
me, cordially pressing her
whopping chest to my regular
chest; and naturally,
indulging openheartedness, I
return her brash, but chummy
advancements.

In the act of agreeably
encircling my arms around the
kitty's abdomen, a slight
gust of wind smacks the left
side of our mutual embrace.

Wasting delay, I,
unaccompanied, probingly
pitch my hyperopia leftward,
and the initial item my far-
sight perceives is an
unfamiliar, carambola-yellow
vessel, docked five-frontward
transports away from my
vulnerable conveyance.

Lucidly, I highly consider
that this tropically xanthic
contraption must be the busty
kitten's means of conveyance.

Discounting the clear-cut
likelihood that she is the
vibrant component of a ploy,
I grant my powerful
attentiveness, entirely, to
the naïve kitten.

Staring deeply in to her
emerald-green eyes, whilst
she relentlessly, but
compassionately stares in to
mine, I lovingly finger-comb
the kitty's shoulder-
brushing, blonde locks, and
untruthfully blandish her
usage of cosmetics.

In a carnal whim, hopelessly
ensnared by my artfully
bewitching impetus, the
kitten imposes her lips to my
lips, and propels her tongue
in to my mouth.

Sustaining my open conduct, I
passionately requite the
kitten's tonguely invasion of
my head's major orifice; and
a mutual, soul-kissing affair
is initiated.

I pleasantly realize that the
downpour, splashing at, and
on, my jacket's rear,
trousers' legs, and manmade
feet, is superbly
complementing the kitty's
spine-tingling *bimbo
hospitality*.

My desire, the august desire
to mightily coax this pasty
specimen in to entering my
solace, and permitting me to,
one by one, blissfully *delve*
its pantie voids, is
inflaming ever greatly with
each lapsing nanosecond.

私は

A minor stiffness *pokes* my
left thigh.

And the kitty, weakly
quivering, breathers our
snogging affair.

THE KITTEN:
"You are such an excellent
kisser, mister..."

"I feel as though that I am
about to ejaculate"

Thereupon, devoting its manly
hands, coarsely affording its
chitchat a hiatus, the feebly
trembling male-kitten grabs
my head firmly, and continues
to intensely soul-kiss my
face's lipped opening.

I suddenly identify that my
transport's canopy has
fastened.

I forcefully strive to remove
myself from the male-kitten's
grasp to investigate.

But, alas, the male-kitty's
unrestrained inferno, in
toto, has engulfed it.

The unanticipated, humble
ruckus of my transport's
cockpit reopening triggers
the male-kitten to fretfully
countermand its lips and
tongue from my labia.

Horribly unnerved, the male-
kitten clinches my right hand
and forearm, and ganders at
the transport in unwavering
preoccupation, and I do the
equivalent, as its canopy
gallivants thru the wet
air...

The accomplished rising of
the Little Kahuna's canopy
fully reveals an irate,
albino bulldyke, discernibly
the male-kitten's, I deem
complicated, teen lover, whom
I instantly suspect is a
fellow frequenter of the
trading post district.

THE BULLDYKE:

"Why were you smooching him,
bitch?!"

"And why are you now clinging
to him?!"

The witlessly shook male-
kitty, wholly adopting
corporeal tautness, hastily
strains to disband it's cushy
cleave.

Sadly, after several tiny
attempts, it seems that the
male-kitty cannot
disassociate itself from my
potent manliness.

Amidst the speechless male-
kitten's inability to sever
its clingy attachment to me,
and my nonchalantly utilizing
a rain-dampened pocket
handkerchief to wipe a
pathetically unnecessary
amount of makeup from my
face, the bulldyke's ire
disturbingly triplicates.

MY THOUGHT:
"Shouldn't *I* be the angry
one?"

I laugh.

Immediately, succeeding my
slope in to a curbed bout of
laughter, the abominably
irate bulldyke, holding her
protruding, jade raincoat-
ensconced tummy, snippily
springs on to the sidewalk,
and uproots a lazer pistol
from her trousers.

Rashly placing her live
lazerarm to the male-kitten's
brow, the appealingly
thickset bulldyke,
undoubtedly of pirate
descent, savagely employs its
function.

The bulldyke, mortifyingly
panicked at the comprehension
of her impulsive move,
scrambles in horror to cull
the male-kitten's marred body
from the sidewalk's concrete.

Canoodling her lover's
defaced corpse, the bulldyke
commences to regretfully
celebrate.

All at once, alongside the
unbearable noise of the
bulldyke's cheerless
interjections of excitement,
a nosey trove of my
neighbors, effeminate males,
of a socially intolerable
variety, women, of a socially
intolerable variety, and
children, of an endearingly
impressionable variety, spurt
from their next-door rooms.

The minute the meddlesome
throng and I totally heave
our visions in to the doing
of witnessing the bulldyke's
haplessly expanding plunge in
to heart-break, the male-
kitten's identification
wristband outsets to project
a polychromatic, holographic
orb, showcasing an expiration
transmission.

THE EXPIRATION TRANSMISSION:

"The ex-wearer of this
identification wristwear has
wholly merged with the
macrocosm..."

"If an ideal citizen, or
ideal citizens, beheld this
merging, and deem what they
beheld 'distressing', please
safeguard the feminized-
masculine deceased, and await
communal-defender sponsored:
*Intangible Trauma
Treatments...*"

"The closest available,
aforementioned terra-
defending authorities will
arrive to amass you, and the
stiff, in approximately
thirty-seconds..."

Ensuing the guilt-ridden
bulldyke's unmistakably
brusque fathoming of the
reiterating, expiration
transmission, she rams her
weapon in to her buccal
cavity, serenely respires,
and impels a fragmentary
percentage of her cranium's
fillings on to her
surroundings.

Anon, in the wake of the
pregnant bulldyke's
checkmate, the crowded
sidewalk is grossly raided by
an appalling disarray.

I apprehend that sirens are
approaching our locus.

I behold the rainfall,
escalating and escalating;
teeming heavier and heavier,
is purging the gore.

I command my transport to
wholly decontaminate, then
promptly deactivate.

I command Kali to vamoose in
to our room, wholly reclaim
her cleanliness, and acquire
hibernation in her 'serenity
crate'.

Blithely grinning, I
relaxingly sit on to the
sidewalk, and assume the
emotional and cerebral rank
of an objectively coiled
cohuatl.

I study a blood-brushed faction of my estranged neighbors, weeping, and bellowing at the top of their lungs, collectively decreeing that they should have never subjected themselves, and their children, to this class of week's end-morning revelations.

I study the rival faction of my blood-grazed estranged neighbors, amid their unified *last hurrah*, taking advantage of our residences' considerate altitude.

This atmosphere is believable to me, nonetheless; I have endured bleaker.

I occupy material liberty, up until a generous, terra-class patrolling transport hovers aloft, and nine, heavily-armed, heavily-armoured, communal defender's rappel to secure the vicinity...

"TRAVEL TREASURES"
旅行刈り取る宝

MY THOUGHT:

"In my book, nothing surpasses a complimentary daytrip..."

I laugh.

Even when still wholly stupefied by the fear-provoking adventus of spontaneous adventure, I laugh.

MY THOUGHTS:

"And to think, if I'd played the wiser, I could have had sex with an unborn baby, a bulldyke, *and* a ladyboy..."

I capitulated to auditors,
amongst a thought scan,
interconnected with a
simultaneous, and as I later
laughterly discovered,
illusionary seven-hour
interrogation, an
encyclopædic seascape of what
I saw, and a matched
narrative of what I knew.

I am definite that my
neighbors, the remorseful
minority, and their
developing offspring, have
also calmly accepted
comparable treatments.

In sync with my heedful
daydreaming, a shapely,
female defender passes the
bench that I am seated on and
disposes herself at a nearby
vacant desk.

Perkily settled, the defender
summarily attends to me.

THE DEFENDER:
"How long have you been
sitting there, sir?"

I:
"Not that long, madam..."

"That auditor, at that desk
over there, advised me, five
minutes ago, to remain here
while he archived my
endorsements"

THE DEFENDER:
"Well, if you would kindly
avow an admissible name, I
can consult the archive to
clarify if you are now
cleared for release"

Enthusiastically, the pretty,
useful defender anticipates
my response.

I:

"My name is *Hoku*..."

"*Hoku Mana*"

THE DEFENDER:

"Wow, that name sounds rather exotic..."

"If you do not mind my asking, what are the meanings and origins of such handles?"

The flirty defender smiles.

I grin.

I:

"My personal name, *ho-koo*, means: *Star*..."

"And my recognized family name, *mah-nah,* means: *Power*..."

"As for their origins, my *makuakāne*, my *baba*, was full-blooded Hawai'ian, Polynesian"

I:

"Although, if you ever were
to catch a shine of my baba,
through the convenient lens
of ignorance, you'd most
likely have the propensity to
exclusively associate him
with African heredity..."

"Due to the condition that
his skin was, often, at first
glance, regarded as sable as
night, like yours, pretty
madam"

Comprehending my frank words
of flattery, the defender
brandishes a sincerely
gladdened face.

Moments after obtaining a lesson on how to correctly spell my etherical brands, the defender deduces, via a holographic, touch-responsive, desktop computer monitor, that I am discharged from defender custody.

THE DEFENDER:
"Sir, we now have clearance to vacate this defender zone"

I:
"We?"

THE DEFENDER:
"Yes, sir..."

"I was predesignated to accompany you home"

I laugh.

The defender chaperons me to
the nearest teleportation
deck, where, under her
continued lenient governance,
she and I, with not an iota
of procrastination, proceed
to teleport in to our
currently embraced defender
zone's civilian docking bay.

Completely teleported in to
the civilian docking bay, the
defender gestures my
awareness to a lonely, two-
passenger patrolling
transport, docked proximus to
the bay's exit.

Swiftly, once more opposing
deferral, the defender and I
tread to this companionless,
patrol conveyance, and board
it.

Rhythmically harnessing the patrol transport's activated controls, the multitasking defender applies a non-visible seat restraint to both of our shells, and, by expressly mining residential coordinates from my identification wristband, configures a course for my inner-city room.

With a course securely set for my home's site, the defender thoughtlessly upswings the transport, and speedily breaches the docking bay's outlet.

In the blink of an eye,
thereafter, the tolerably
chatty defender and I
converge on our goal.

The defender, adhering to the
primary phase of parallel-
docking protocol, parallel
hover parks our transport
ahead of my incessantly
feminine-charming, previously
anchored conveyance.

A tick in to the defender's
hover parking, a docking-
stage surfaces and presents
itself to the belly of our
transportation.

The defender gracefully
perches our transport, on to
the eager docking-stage, and
actualizes the levitation of
the lively mechanism's
butterfly doors.

With merriment whelming my
mood, stomping from the
patrol transport's co-pilot's
place, and rambling on to the
unbloodied sidewalk; the
defender drifting from the
transport's pilot's place,
and curiously shadowing my
action, I tune in to
development a buoyant walk to
my room's entrance, priming
to touch my identification
wristwear to its exterior
control panel.

Yet, in the middle of my
lighthearted sauntering, an
indigo hover-horse jets in to
view, from the north, and
docks anterior to the
defender's patrol vehicle;
prompting me to a
standstill...

MOMMA:

"Little baba!!!"

My *makuahine*, my *momma*,
embellished by woody
bifocals, a flamingo pink-
obi-sashed turquoise *yukata*,
and wooden *geta*; a knapsack
aligned with her posterior
thorax; her red, head hairs
unitedly styled in a hoisted
ponytail, leaps from her
hover-horse, and bolts to me.

I:

"Momma, why are you here?"

私は

MOMMA:

"I was doing my darnedest not
to be anxious when you didn't
call me this afternoon, but
then I witnessed an
informative transmission that
proclaimed that a party
suicide had occurred in your
locality..."

"I attempted to get in touch
with you, but I discovered
that your identification
wristband's communication
capabilities were being
temporarily inhibited..."

"So, I contacted an ally of
mine, and, luckily, they were
able to put me at ease"

Spontaneously, finally
choosing to comprehend my
question, momma is angered.

MOMMA:

"I was worried loopy about
you, Hoku!"

"And you have the audacity to
question why I'm here?!"

Momma, peaking her parental
harassments, acknowledges
that a defender is dallying
at my side.

THE DEFENDER:
"Osiyo, ma'am..."

MOMMA:
"Who are you?"

THE DEFENDER:
"I am Communal Defender
Ahyoka Ayes"

MOMMA:
"Oki-doki, it's nice to meet
you, defender..."

"I is Lady Yuki Mana"

Momma and the defender
exchange sociable gazes.

Momma, reissuing her benevolent energies to her regretfully reachable son, leers at me, with no dissolution in sight for her renowned coddling.

MOMMA:

"Are you hungry, my *hokey pokey* boy?"

Aloofly imagining that the beauty mark on momma's Scottish-Japanese jowl is challenging me to a glaring contest, I verbally advance nothing to her passé babying.

Momma, angered by my
unfailing disinterest in her
overprotection, lunges at me,
and snatches my jacket's
zipper-joined threads, and
struggles to shake me, like
the short, chubby, wide-
hipped, saggy-breasted
lunatic she is, that I, so
fondly, throughout my thirty-
two years of sentience, had
grown a rich rapport with.

MOMMA:

"Answer me, Hoku!"

"Are you hungry?!"

"Yes or no?!"

"Just because you *think* that
you are a seasoned adult,
does not mean I am not your
momma anymore!"

Whilst my spry, nonagenarian mom persistently *tries* to shake an attentive response out of me, I eye the adorably lingering defender, and smirk, unfazed.

I:
"Would you care to dine with us?"

The pokerfaced defender palpates her hips, and slowly, but decisively, considers my genial invitation...

"DÉJÀ VU"
すでに見

Properly provoking girlishly
receptive them to feel
welcome in my modestly regal
apartment, subsequent my
cloaking my disinfected
nudity with an apricot pajama
outfit; subsequent a private,
unclothed episode of head-to-
toe decontamination, once I
conveniently jettison my
unwanted boots, choker, and
clothes, in to my fore door-
adjacent recycle bin, and
unworriedly exit my bathroom,
I individually prepare,
distribute, and jointly sip
agave nectar-sweetened tea,
and commence to openly
disclose to my invitee, and
mom, the explicit details of
my morning experience.

As I begin to viscerally
divulge the *nitty-gritty* of
it, mom decides that she does
not want to consume my true
tale, any longer.

Impulsively, momma tidies my
bed, babbling on about *usual
bed untidiness* as she did so,
and opts to migrate to the
kitchen space of the room;
together with three, jobless
tea bowls.

Momma, jawing on about my
usual breastmilk fetish, and
my *usual restaurant
addiction*; unveiling her
daily disparagements of the
diverse, wee-bit
supplemented, eatery leaflets
that are decking my milk-
stocked refrigerator,
announces that tonight she
will be concocting: *shrimp
ramen noodle soup*.

私は

Momma procures a pot from my
cookware pantry, rinses it,
traps aqua in it, and
arranges it on my oven's
cooktop.

Activating the oven's
cooktop, momma extracts, and,
laconically soliciting I and
the defender's complete
alertness, publicizes an oh-
so familiar collection of
knapsack-unpacked organic
ingredients, and
appropriately marries them to
the heating pot.

With my spellbinding orating at a pause, the defender buries her face in her hands, and quietly sits alone on my sofa, processing the information that I had audibly revealed to her; no doubt.

Meanwhile, I shawl my pajama shirt-hid, flesh-masked clavicles, sternum and humeri with a nap blanket, loll in my armchair, affiliate a reading monocle with my right eye, and engross 'timeless', mint condition, paperback literature that my baba recently gifted me.

MOMMA:

"Defender, why don't you remove your raincape?"

Comprehending momma's mellow invoke, the defender unearths her face, and promptly spots the coat rack, positioned in the corner near the room's fore door.

Shifting in to a standing
posture, the defender repels
a brown, informal patrol
raincape from her body, and
adds it to my accommodating
coat rack; leaving an
identification wristband, a
powder-blue sports brassiere,
a holstered lazerarm, brown,
yellow-striped, informal
patrol pants, and black,
metallic, formal patrol boots
to be the articles that
garnish her dark, *theobroma
cacao* figure.

And behind tenderly deducting
her boots, and socks, from
her pretty, sizeable feet,
the defender softly
reinstates her rump to the
sofa.

MOMMA:

"Hoku..."

"Doesn't the defender have an appetizing figure???"

Momma's furthered tactlessness drives me in to an idiotic outburst of laughter; and that idiotic outburst of laughter drives me to unintentionally banish myself to the room's flooring.

Laboring to quash my
unbridled amusement, I aspire
to disable momma's restless
throat.

I:
"Be respectful, momma!!!"

The defender, tamely
giggling, zips to momma's
defense.

THE DEFENDER:
"It is fashionable, sir..."

"It is all 'ight..."

"Your mamma's query sounds of
well will..."

"And I *do* love to hear of
pleasant thoughts, pertaining
to *me*"

Coming to grips with her
mildly narcissistic
endorsement of momma's
predictably unforeseen
inquiry, I, abruptly, conceal
my glee, and request the
defender to charitably poise
to resting attention...

The enthusiastically handsome
defender's head hair is
black, woolly, and boyishly
lovely.

And her ears, directly
exposed to my eyesight; in
consequence of added
entreaty, are cutely
attached, and cutely pointed.

Her eyes are bright, ebony,
and goatish; and her
interdepended superciliums
and ciliums are thick and
baby doll-like.

The lower margins of her
gloriously makeup-lacking
face, are immaculately
containing caress-worthy,
low, zygomatic bones, and a
fittingly strong mandible.

Her nose is wide and
adorable, and her lips are
full and suggestive.

And her smile, elicited by my
inherent knack for
charismatic foolishness,
dazzlingly features spaced,
central upper incisors.

The defender, in my
unexpressed *mana'o*, in my
unexpressed *opinion*,
accurately represents a
twenty-two-year-old, or more
possibly, twenty-three-year-
old, average built, average
heighted, systematic,
satisfied, virago of
exceedingly undeniable,
unforced, feminine potency.

The defender's arms are
arched, and at her waistline,
of which I estimate has a
circumference of twenty-six,
her aptly manicured, almond
finger-nailed hands are
situated on her hips, of
which I guesstimate have a
circumference of thirty-
eight.

Briefly surveying the
defender's *heso,* and
incarcerated *oppai*, I
confidently discern that it
is an outie, and expertly
deem that they are F cups.

Humoring a hunch, I blatantly
ask the defender if she is
synthetic. And she responds,
unequivocally, owning that
title.

I sense a change.

Abandoning the defender, I
pull myself up from the
floor, and glide in to the
kitchen.

I stumble upon a handwritten
note, on the front and back
of paper, lying on the
kitchen table.

THE NOTE:

"Dear Hoku, I is journeying
home, my baby.

I apologize for not
announcing my intentions of
ghosting you, but I did not
want to interrupt.

Anywho, I advocate that you
permit the defender to stay
with you and keep you safe
for the night. And to ensure
that you authorize her to do
just that, I have taken her
raincape home to launder it."

THE NOTE:

"I know that you have a combined washer and dryer appliance, but, as is true, from my view, with machines that have a distinct purpose, my washer and dryer appliances are more intimate with their individual roles, and are therefore, more effective.

Enjoy the soup.

Love, Momma :)

P.S., I took the liberty of amassing your blood-stained clothes, choker, and boots also."

I glance at the defender, as
we are eating dinner,
together at my darling
kitchen table, and I am
afflicted with severe
promnesia.

THE DEFENDER:
"What is the perplexity,
sir?"

"Never shared a meal with a
replicant like *me* before?"

Evanescently expelling
fanatical giggles, ably
clasping her copper
chopsticks, the defender
renews the gluttonous
assailing of her copper soup
bowl.

Withholding myself,
momentarily, from
entertaining the piggish,
synthetic defender's jabber,
I consume water from my
copper cup.

THE DEFENDER:

"Do you have any alcohol,
sir?"

I:

"Yes, madam..."

"There are various synth-wine
bottles in the cabinet, below
the sink, behind you"

I climax my gentle discourse.

And the defender leaves the
table, and softly raids the
kitchen sink's underling
cabinet.

Confiscating a premium pick,
the defender giggles,
nestling the five-liter
bottle dearly to her chest,
and ambles backward to her
seat.

Child-like, the defender
positions her soup bowl to
her maw, and in an eagle
speed, gobbles the remainder
of her soup, uncorks the
synthetic wine bottle, and
replaces the emptiness of her
bowl with synth wine.

The defender wafts at the
fragrant, replicant wine. And
once again, she swiftly
renders her bowl *unfilled*.

Joining her in an epic
extravaganza of successive
swiggin', I and the defender,
the defender and I,
surprisingly, deepen our
acquaintance...

"MASCULINE, FEMININE, REPEAT"
男性的、女性的、リピート

I startlingly awake, upon my platform bedstead-lain, neatly layered bedding-disguised, queen-sized mattress, hangover-free, and shirtless.

Whereas shirtless, the lower half of my flesh is enshrouded by footed, pajama trousers.

I awake to the sight of sofa-lazed Ms. Ayes, whose swarthy silkiness is garnished with informal patrol pants, an identification wristband, and a wireless, sports brassiere.

Extending further respect to my, now, soundly snoozing guest, noticing that I must have neglected to coherently allot it to her, afore I was stealthily commandeered by sleep, I erect myself from inactivity, seize my nap blanket, and gently fling it on to her.

Succeeding a much-needed
session of urination, wherein
my splendid toilet dutifully
situated forth a see-through
tube to the head of my
morning wood, and *very*
interestingly stimulated
urine from it, I vacate my
bathroom, swan to my window,
and, subjecting myself to a
preview of today's
unrepressed sunlight,
segregate my windowpane's
draperies.

Revisiting slumbering Ms.
Ayes, I fruitfully try to
wake her by viciously blowing
at her nose.

Wholly exposing her vision to
my prettiness, after
voluntarily blinking her
eyelids thrice, Ms. Ayes
flirtatiously laughs.

Now mirroring me, as she
knowingly lazes, vivaciously,
the Ms. flashes an
openhearted smile.

MS. AYES:

"Good day, Mr. Mana"

I:

"Good day to you, Ms."

MS. AYES:

"I would like to bathe, now,
afore I fly..."

"If you are okay with me
committing to the doing of
utilizing your bathing space,
that is"

I:

"You are still my guest 'til
your cape arrives, Ms. Ayes,
so it is not a problem..."

"There are towels and wash
cloths in the hoard closet
that my bathroom embraces..."

"And in my shower cabin, and
at my sink, is a hygiene-
solution dispenser..."

"In addition, my shower
cabin's shower-head, and my
sink's faucet, spray and
temperature water in
accordance to verbalized
demand"

I:

"And if you decide to make use of my toilet, do not be alarmed if, promptly afterward, it proposes to pamper your genitalia, anus, and perineum"

MS. AYES:

"Mr. Mana, you really know how to engender a synth sister to feel comfy"

Ms. Ayes giggles.

I grin.

MS. AYES:

"When I am showering, if it doesn't trouble you, Mr. Mana, could you go out to my transport's cargo-hold, and annex a duffle bag from it?"

Employing her identification wristwear, the Ms. commands her transport's cargo-hold to unseal.

MS. AYES:

"I should have brought in my standby-clothing duffle myself, last night, when I remembered I had it..."

"But I did not want my momentary absence to hamper our fun"

Ms. Ayes deploys a rewarding operation of standing apart from her dwindled unconsciousness and shifts to the bathroom in an effortless enchantment.

I:
"Are you reporting for duty today, Ms.?"

Ms. Ayes opens the bathroom's door; then, ever more starry-eyed than afore now, she proceeds to smile at me, radiantly.

MS. AYES:
"For me..."

"Today happens to be the start of a leave of truancy"

Ms. Ayes enters the bathroom. And unhurriedly, closes its door.

The Ms., applying a puissant tone, provokes the shower cabin's shower-head to outpour...

Reveling in the second,
inaugural rite of my numerous
weekbegan morning rituals, I
pilfer a pint carton of milk
from my refrigerator, loll on
my sofa, and order my room's
virtual hostess to project,
directly on to my cerebrum's
sight, sound, and smell
processors, this week's
published installment of my
much-loved, anime series.

Yet, for unpinpointed
reasons, alike last night;
when Ms. Ayes respectfully
requested that a specific
composition of contemporary
music be played openly, my
room's virtual hostess will
not respond to direction, no
matter how platonically they
are beseeched to participate
in a diplomatic conversation.

Contradictory to my weekbegan
desire to value a short
episode of animations,
merrily guzzling milk, I
curtly stroll outside to
appropriate Ms. Ayes's duffle
bag.

Executing my hospitable
initiative, I retreat in to
my room with the Ms.'s
duffle. And I and it
restfully assemble at my
kitchen table.

As her insentient duffle bag
and I attain relaxation at
the kitchen table, I
encounter Ms. Ayes's
lazerarm, sheltered, and
resting on the table's top.

Intent on inspecting it, I
detach this lethal tech from
its asylum.

I confess, to you, upfront,
that I am not necessarily a
lethal-technology aficionado.

But, thru abbreviated
observation, I determine that
Ms. Ayes's lethal tech is
indeed the identical lazerarm
fingered by that commendably
plucky, ladyboy-impregnated
bulldyke who yesterday, I
recall, failed to pinch my
little ship.

This popular, handheld,
electromagnetically powered
lazerarm, cautiously cradled
in my hands, is a product of
a hauntingly well-known
conglomerate.

Whilst I am restoring her
weapon to its shelter, Ms.
Ayes, afresh, exercises her
vocal authority, and the
shower cabin's spouting
shower-head turns deaf.

Mobilizing commonsense and
consideration, I tote Ms.
Ayes's duffle to the
bathroom's door.

Toggling open the bathroom's
entrance, in harmonious
sequence to my knocking at
it, the toweled Ms. praises
my furthered generosities.

Suddenly, and upsettingly,
there goes a familiar
progression of soft rapping
at my fore door.

I sluggishly rush to the door
and open it.

The door competently clambers
to show my momma, mainly
bejeweled by the chic,
sophisticated coupling of an
azul *yukata*, and a black-and-
amarillo-checkered *obi* sash.

Momma is minorly upraised by
geta, and her rojo mane,
prettified with a duet of
azul *heddoheasutikku*, is cast
in a bun; and prettifying her
ears, and prettifying her
matured, girly visage, are
diamond earrings, and woody
bifocals.

In her left hand, momma is
grasping an open, foldable
fan, and in her right hand,
she is grasping a laundry
bag.

Momma stares at me, fanning herself, playfully.

MOMMA:

"Ohayou, little baba..."

"Where is the defender?"

"Did you two fornicate all night?"

And before momma can further her joshing, I grouchily shut my door.

A DEEP, FEMALE VOICE:

"Mr. Mana!"

"You should not be treating your mamma that way!"

I optically acquaint myself with a fully-clothed, and a fully-infuriated, Ms. Ayes.

I:

"How do you know that it is my momma?"

MS. AYES:

"Do I look visionless to you, Mr. Mana?!"

"As my duffle and I were exiting your bathroom, I observed leftward, and I plainly saw her standing in the doorway!"

MY THOUGHT:

"How in the hells did the Ms. Ayes get dressed that fast?"

Now, I recognize that Ms. Ayes's presence is greatly stimulating mine sensitivities.

Broadening my analyzation of this phenomenon, I glare vigorously at my enraged ex-guest.

Quickly, with the steadfast advent of my intolerance for her presently domineering attitude, the Ms.'s infuriation fades; and tersely, she humbly pleads for my forgiveness.

I infer that it is not the feistiness that this Ms. had put in to her scolding that has overwhelmed me.

I infer that this Ms.'s classy, feminine attire, consisting of teal penny loafers, a teal wristlet handbag, and a flattering, teal sundress, is not the root of this increased stirring in my core.

However, as I persist my
transient, but thoroughly
insightful prying, I
ultimately conclude that my
increased stimulation is
stemming from the further
realization that this Ms., a
high-grade replicant Ms. whom
I meekly met yesterday, *is*.

Relinquishing bubbly pity to
Ms. Ayes, applauding her
sustained, stunning, and *all-
natural*, womanly upkeep, I
unhurriedly re-open my fore
door...

"NEVER DIE."
決して死なない

Momma, angered by my declining her proposal that we found a trio, and have breakfast at the most superlative restaurant of my, now, one hundred and eighty favorite city restaurants, to thankfully exalt Ms. Ayes for her overnight defender duty, which, wonderfully, in retrospect, she overbearingly and inventively prompted to nocturnally disturb my habitual reclusion, incites a protest about my daily refusal to consume first meal; until, somehow, lingering Ms. Ayes sways her to innerstand that preferring to deny first meal isn't a dreadful occurrence, after all.

Noting a flowering suspicion
that she is plotting to do
her best, this week's
beginning; in person, to
successfully see to it that I
am not free to gain from the
hallowed services of brothel
dwelt prostitutes, which she
indisputably knows I
religiously do each
weekbegan, indiscriminately,
'til nightfall, I allow momma
and the Ms. to socialize
amongst themselves, afore I
supremely expel them from my
room.

Concurrently, I wholly bathe
myself.

And afterwards, leisurely
accessing my bathroom's,
predominantly wardrobe-
comprising, hoard closet, I
tittivate myself with:
Prince-purple crotchless
panties, Prince-purple cargo
trousers, a Prince-purple
long-sleeved henley, Prince-
purple ankle socks, and,
lastly, casual boots that
happen to be Prince-purple.

I spritz lavandula perfume on
to my collar and wrists, then
spritz peppermint breath-
sweetener, twice, in to my
oral cavity, then suavely
analyze my donned,
glamorously incomplete,
purple ensemble in my adult
floor mirror; when, finally
desiring to conversate,
Halle, my virtual hostess,
authoritatively, sensitively,
materializes in to my
perceptible experience as, as
what I had gingerly
programmed her to be; the
very day I moved in to my
room, an ever exquisitely
clad, human-sized, fresh-
faced, wingless, flat-
breasted, female pixie, and
coolly airs a grievance about
me enabling another feminine
energy, other than my
wonderful momma, to embed
herself in to the apartment,
unannounced.

Halle articulates to me that,
when I strove to introduce
her to my guest; consonant
with what I effectively did
with Kali, while we were
excessively drinking synth
alcohol, and *unwaveringly*
pursuing musical stimuli, she
was so irritated by my

guest's mannish *southern drawl*, and *perkiness*, that she wanted to explicitly berate her with nasty insults, but decided to be uncommunicative because she did not covet the imaginable calculation that I would become drunkenly annoyed with her frankly displaying discontentment.

Adjourning my assuring Halle that, whether I am synthetically intoxicated, or not, an incidence of airing sentiments straightforwardly to my guest, or to a future guest or guests that she disapproves of, wouldn't have changed, and *will not* change, the actuality that I adore her especial, pleasurable assistances, I tittivate my left wrist with my active identification wristwear, complement my long-sleeved henley with a Prince-purple asymmetrical poncho, associate nāga-black sunspecs with my ears and face, and assert my subtle androgyny in to my room's main space.

Straightaway, dexterously and summarily foiling my ousting intents, mom, with trivial aid from her *new gal-pal* 'Ahyoka Ayes', determinedly, but politely persuades me to truly *carpe diem*, and briefly travel to her home, and appreciate the benefits of a homemade second meal in honor of, as bashfully confirmed by her; and heeded, but highly doubted by me, admirer deprived, Ms. Ayes.

And to cruise *ultra-stylishly*, and *ultra-cozily*, advising that individual transports are inappropriate for *our threesome's* journey; consequent my pronouncing that I will be utilizing *my own* vehicle to visit her territory, momma impeccably persuades me in to traveling by the means of her awaiting, luxury transport.

Electing to forfeit my prior plans, totally surrendering myself to this conceivably favorable adventure, I exit my room ahead of momma, and her unquestionably cute, and alive, new friend, and assimilate in to her luxury transportation.

After a snappy voyage,
immaculately enlivened by a
medley of ageless
instrumentals providing
palpable, nostalgic
reinforcement to her
guileless narration of how
she *chose* baba, when she was
a sufficiently prosperous
lemon vendor of sixteen
years, and he was a
productively venturesome,
indefinably impressive,
masculine human of twenty-
four years, momma's luxury
transport pilots over her
estate's arrival gate,
knowledgeably ignoring the
guidance of the enter stretch
of a stony, palm tree-lined,
horseshoe driveway, and
advances to a ground-
established, transport haven.

Momma dwells on the mountainous, southern rural outskirts of the city, in an extravagant, blue five-story home, founded in the midmost of a forty-acre citrus limon orchard, and bordered with a great, golden brick wall.

Alighted in the transport haven, momma, afore she benevolently instigated our evacuation of her luxury transportation, progressively appealed to enthusiastic Ms. Ayes's audible scope, by bragging that her *green fingers* had earned her, and baba's, estate, sixty-six years consecutively, *pick your own lemons* prestige...

Tailing momma right to, and through, her yellow mahogany French doors, in to the wholeheartedly jubilant, ineffably picturesque, divinely odorous foyer of her home, Ms. Ayes is stimulated to heightened enthusiasm.

MS. AYES:
"Lady Yuki, I am nearly wordless!!!"

"This foyer feels, looks, and smells *so* beautiful!!!"

Unreservedly giggling, the enjoyably childish Ms. warmly grasps my hands, and strives to provoke me in to dancing about with her.

Granted that I do not typically reap pleasure from dancing vertically, once more, I see no other choice but to indulge Ms. Ayes's wholesome frolicking.

Eloquently, smirking, momma disbands Ms. Ayes and I's silly dancing.

MOMMA:

"This is merely nothing, my
dear, Ahyoka..."

Wholly restraining herself,
Ms. Ayes, gently unhanding my
clammy hands, slowly, but
eagerly pivots to momma.

MOMMA:

"This foyer...”

“This home...”

“It is just a sheer reminder"

Momma suddenly mimics
quietness, as tears begin
escaping her eyes.

Innerstanding what momma has
acknowledged, I kindly guide
Ms. Ayes to the front room.

Entered in to the front room,
I demote my paper-thin
sunspecs to a trouser pocket,
and beckon the Ms.'s
interests to a noteworthy,
platinum-enclosed photograph,
hanging above the room's
fireplace.

The legendary photograph
shows my comely, expecting
momma, boasting ruddy
ringlets, and boasting a
burgundy strapless evening
gown, swathed in the
machismo, but delicate, upper
limbs of my baba, Bhaskar
Mana.

My biologically baby-faced
baba, whose left ear is
ornamented with a modest
golden hoop, and whose head
hair is proudly fashioned in
his signature 'mellow
warrior' dreadlocks, is
decorously attired in a
scarlet-enhanced, white
tuxedo.

MS. AYES:

"Where is your baba now, Mr. Mana?"

I:

"He is dead, Ms. Ayes..."

"As of today, he died two weeks ago"

On the defensive, momma fearsomely darts in to the front room, and scornfully opposes my cheerless assertions.

MOMMA:

"Hoku!"

"Your baba is not dead!"

"You hear me?!"

"We are him, damn it!"

Abruptly ashamed of her tactless, sorrowful voicings, momma calmly places her hands over her heart.

Possessing no effective rebuttal to crush her factual claims, I ably toddle to momma, and weepily bow to her.

Unsurprisingly, momma
reverently palms the sides of
my face, and apologetically,
consolingly, kisses my
forehead.

Conspicuously bolstering
momma and I's mournful
standings, awkwardly dropping
to her knees, Ms. Ayes begins
to cry, nosily.

Consequent bestowing one
final repentant kiss to my
brow, momma benevolently
moves to the sobbing, knelt
Ms., and maternally comforts
her.

MOMMA:

"Hoku..."

"It would make me happier if you were to give Ahyoka a small tour of the workshop, afore we have lunch"

Momma reviews an embarrassed Ms. Ayes's teary eyes.

MOMMA:

"You are greatly worthy, dear..."

"And what is great about your worth is that *you know*"

And with that declared, momma benignly withdraws from the room...

"PRIVATE"
プライベート

I hurry, akin to a hasty
monkey, from the last step of
the foyer's descending
stairwell, and unify with the
whelming blackness of the
unlit basement.

Attempting to feel my way to
the basement's light switch,
jokingly vexed, I look to Ms.
Ayes.

And, surprise, surprise, my
glance hits upon total
darkness.

I hear Ms. Ayes giggle.

And the lights turn on.

I:
"Very much ta, Ms...."

"As I am sure you overheard,
I was very much struggling"

I laugh.

MS. AYES:
"*'A'ole pilikia*, *no problem*,
Mr. Mana..."

"I innerstand"

A giggly Ms. Ayes tenderly
shoves a stunned me.

In response to her responding
to me in my third native,
absolute favored, preserved
tongue, gruffly transmitting
my concentration elsewhere, I
intentionally ignore
flirtatious Ms. Ayes, and
wander to a workbench-
reposed, open, hoard box.

Instantly seeking to
repossess my attentiveness, a
query fleetly captures Ms.
Ayes's curiosity.

MS. AYES:

"Mr. Mana..."

"Could you refresh my
memory?"

"Can you divulge to me
exactly what you do, again,
day-to-day, to attract
perpetual currency?"

Frontally engaging Ms. Ayes's
artificial interest, I put my
hands at my midriff, and
smile at her, brightly.

I:

"I am a refurbisher, and
dealer, of a very wide array
of broken and junked items,
Ms...."

"And, along with fourteen
older sisters, their clans,
and an extremely unreachable,
ex-defender, Irish twin
brother, and mom, I am a
presiding beneficiary of my
baba's corporation..."

"But, before you ask what our
conglomerate manufactures,
permit me to demonstrate"

Engrossing the hoard box,
quickly browsing its
inventory, vividly projected
directly on to my cerebrum,
I, virtually, tap my teamed
left middle and pointer-
finger twice on the labelled
image of the compactly stored
artifact that I want to
displace; and I am tangibly
reacquainted with my baba's
cherished, earliest
successful, lazer assault
rifle.

I squeeze the lazer assault
rifle's grip, one time, to
render it *live*, and I rest
its wooden buttstock in my
left shoulder pocket, and,
whilst narrowing my sight, I
aim its beaded muzzle at a
transparent, gelatinlike
mannequin, furnished with
lifelike bodily fixings, and
sited to the fore of a
segment of projectile-
absorbent wall, twenty-five
yards from my stance.

Impatiently, I apply a steady
grasp to the live lazerarm's
grip, and sloppily sanction a
cascade of lethal lazers to
burst from its stubby muzzle.

Cheerfully, I cease my
compression of the quick-fire
lazer rifle, and, afore I
accurately deposited the
archaic lethal tech back in
to the hoard box, I watch the
barely marred mannequin
regenerate.

MS. AYES:
"That was a fantastic
demonstration, Mr. Mana..."

"But, now it is my go"

Ms. Ayes reaches in to her
wristlet handbag, and,
spectacularly, pulls out a
mini lazerarm; unambiguously,
a mini lazerarm duly credited
to my baba's unstifled
imagination.

MS. AYES:

"This little one is the first lazerarm that my daddy taught me how to shoot..."

The Ms. giggles.

MS. AYES:

"I label it 'Nuttah'"

Briskly flaunting her defender's marksmanship, the Ms. deftly aims her live lazerarm, and heartlessly squeezes it, repeatedly, devastating the inanimate mannequin's essential, bodily characteristics, in spot-on curt blasts...

Tenderly snubbing my plea for
an encore, her interest
fleetly captured by an
additional query, Ms. Ayes
conceals her proven,
miniature lazerarm.

MS. AYES:
"Is your family's corporation
solely a lethal-technology
manufacturer, Mr. Mana?"

I:
"My baba was an obsessive
polymath, Ms...."

I exhale nosily.

I:
"So, the answer to your
question is a *no*"

I:

"My baba skillfully toyed
with, practically, *the whole
shebang* when it came to
coagulating innovations..."

"Though, second to
occasionally offering frank
and humorous growth advices,
solidifying weapons was his
foremost addiction"

Humorlessly, I turn away from
Ms. Ayes.

And I, anew, exploit the
hoard box.

Forth from the jolly old
hoard box, I spiritedly
displace a six-inch by
twenty-four-inch metallic
hilt. And wasting no second,
I grip the bladeless hilt
tenaciously, and a curved,
incandescent, orange, long
blade penetrates the upward
air.

Brusquely unhanding the hilt,
restoring its blade to
dormancy, I cockily glare at
an astonished Ms. Ayes.

私は

As a hilariously vocal Ms.
Ayes seeks to recoup, on the
workbench's stool, from the
incredible spectacle of my
one-of-a-kind, glowing,
lengthy, lethal phallus, I
seek a weapons belt.

Confidently exploring the
beloved hoard box's limitless
inventory, one last time; for
today, I rediscover a weapons
belt, hidden in a black box
that virtually bore the
label: 'For Hoku's iaido long
blade'.

I situate the recovered
weapons belt, comfortably at
my waist, and reintroduce its
retractable wire's magnetic
tip to the base of my weapon.

Afore signaling a still
laughterly thunderstruck Ms.
Ayes to follow me up the
stairs, to pursue further
nourishments, I blissfully
test the persisted utility of
my weapons belt by
outreaching my magnetically
associated lethal tech with
unrestricted ease...

"THIS."

これ。

I ready to exercise my larynx to loudly expel the enunciation of *momma*, but a wildly circulating, delectable stench halts the tangible formation of my mighty, conceptual holla.

Consequently, I and Ms. Ayes corporally teleport ourselves to the locale, and source, of the prevalent, mouthwatering stink.

MOMMA:

"Oh, rich!!!"

"I was just about to call for y'all..."

"I guess the aroma beat me to it"

Momma, posted in her
majestic, main dining room
table's head chair,
encourages our increasingly
uprising thirsts, and
appetites, by pouring, from
one of three personal
pitchers, freshly homemade
pineapple mint *remoneedo* in
to a glass cup, then
gratifyingly drinking from
that glass cup, then
sniffing, then satisfyingly
nibbling on, a slice of a
thin-crust, extra-large,
eighteen-inch, square-cut,
freshly homemade pineapple
and grilled ham *piza*.

MOMMA:
"Come, come..."

"Stop gawking like hungry
dumb asses, and pop a squat"

Gratefully reacting to
momma's jesting, Ms. Ayes and
I adopt our reserved,
shoulder dining chairs.

Ensuing a heartfelt
thanksgiving, excellently led
by silence, I forget who, and
what, I am, and eat and drink
in rapido timing, granting
momma, nor the Ms., an even
chance to ingest their
portions of *piza* and
remoneedo afore I ingest
mine.

Nonetheless, shockingly, Ms.
Ayes has, apparently, bid
farewell to the independences
of her portions, also.

MS. AYES:

"Finished your lunching, Mr. *gluttonous* Mana?"

The Ms. teasingly giggles.

I:

"Why yes, I have finished my lunching, Ms. *unflawed* Ayes..."

"And, if I may ask, have you finished *yours*?"

The Ms., momentarily implementing a kissable hand to move my notice back to her unemployed dining utensils, lightheartedly scoffs at *my* needless inquiry.

MS. AYES:

"Clearly, Mr. Mana..."

"You can perceive that truth"

Identifying the birthplace of Ms. Ayes and I's frisky banter, momma snickers, covering her mouth in the prime of her testudine-paced mastication.

MOMMA:
"Something tells me, Ahyoka, that you and my Hoku would make an exceptional couple..."

"Thus, since you've both wordfully admitted aloud that you've finished lunching, why don't you two visit the cinema for an after-lunch date?"

Expectant of our oral reactions, eccentrically, mom grins at a pokerfaced Ms. Ayes, then grins at a collectedly anxious I.

Ms. Ayes, now perceptibly
skittish, prettily ascents
from her dining chair.

MS. AYES:
"Lady Yuki, I desire to wash
my dining utensils to
manifest my gratefulness"

MOMMA:
"Oki-doki, dear..."

"You do that..."

"The kitchen is through that
doorsill, to the left"

Spoiling procrastination, a
relieved Ms. Ayes vanishes.

I:

"Damn it, momma..."

"Why is my heart being abnormally stimulated by Ms. Ayes's attendance?"

"What is wrong with me?"

Momma, gayly grinning, pauses her lunching.

MOMMA:

"You are in love, Hoku..."

"Plain, and simple"

Momma, studiously continuing her lunching, carelessly laughs.

I:

"No doubt, momma, no doubt..."

"Yet, I do not think I could unwaveringly couple with Ms. Ayes if I find that she is a *practiced* volva..."

"You know very well that I admire their impeccable truths, as I admire your impeccable advices, but, contrary to my booming desire to commence an orgy with an assorted gaggle of them now, I have honestly become dissatisfied with that pretty variety, entirely"

I exhale noisily.

MOMMA:

"Hoku, 'lax your judgements..."

"And *pa'a ka waha*, *observe, listen, and learn*, so that I can finish my turtle-paced lunching"

Momma and I, simultaneously, vent untamed glee...

"MOVIE WOO"

映画宇

Ms. Ayes softly returns from the kitchen.

MS. AYES:
"Are we heeding your momma's advice, or not, Mr. Mana?"

The Ms.'s soothing voicings sharply extricate me from contemplation.

I:
"Certainly, my charming acquaintance..."

"We are visiting the damned cinema..."

"Now, thoughtfully help I up from this chair, afore I thoughtfully changes my mind"

Positively struck by their deliveries, momma scores impermanent hilarity from my sarcastic responses, as Ms. Ayes snappily abets me to my feet.

Momma, smirking at unsmiling
I and simpering Ms. Ayes's
ephemerally standing next to
each other, hastily tenders
forth a mandate.

MOMMA:

"Pilot *the mistress*, Hoku"

Partially dumbfounded, I
heartily laugh at momma's
illogical instruction.

I:

"Momma, why would you think
that I and my date would
desire to pilot a *car*?"

Urgently, fleetingly
disregarding mom's presence,
I whisper in to Ms. Ayes's
right ear.

I:

"If you have not previously
known of such, baby girl, a
car is a mode of olden
transportation that should be
wholly forgotten"

Seemingly elated by the
reality that I faintly
projected enunciations
directly in to my non-
prostitute date's right ear
canal, momma inadvertently
regains my acknowledgements
by eccentrically guffawing.

MOMMA:
"There is no 'why', Hoku..."

"Just do it, and make me
happier, please"

Stomaching my emotionally
adolescent, physically
middle-aged momma's present
expectations of me, the Ms.
and I retire the dining room,
and reinvade the foyer.

And subsequent relevantly
invading its men's and
women's rooms, I and the Ms.
retire the foyer, and move to
the proximate coordinates of
the transport haven.

Punctually, I raise the transport haven's access, and expose, to the light, a bespoke classic luxury transport, a bespoke classic terra-class hover-horse, and, *the mistress* momma absurdly mandated that I pilot, an anciently deluxe, unforgettably purplish-red leather and wood-upholstered, greenish-blue-glazed, four-passenger *sports sedan*.

At my command, Ms. Ayes hurries to the uncovered mistress's co-pilot's door, and seizes its co-pilot's place. And I, somewhat comparably founding my reign of its pilot's place, compress the mistress's squeeze-to-start *steering wheel*, and furiously *put the pedal to the metal*.

Shortly, discriminating that the mistress is closely and steadfastly progressing toward its guard, the estate's departure gateway dynamically endorses our exodus.

By way of my baba's, and my
momma's, prudently instilled
car-piloting knowledges, on
the heels of a brief lecture
on how to buckle a *safety
belt*; a comical element of
car etiquette that sped in to
remembrance a trice ago, I,
and the inspiringly
enthusiastic Ms. Ayes, safely
forsake rural roads, and
pierce city limits on the
ground level.

Marginally assisted by a
present-day GPS, prizing the
amusing regards that our
wheeled, ground-hugging
chariot is progressively
amassing from bystanders, I
smoothly maneuver to the
ground level's main street,
and, with its flamboyantly
luring neon sign now in my
far-sighted eye view,
confidently localize an
outwardly superlative cinema.

I pilot to the marvelously
alluring cinema's placement,
and boldly veer left, clear
of its minimally occupied
landing area, and, with the
aspiration of securing
seclusion for the mistress to
bask in, hurriedly roll in to
an adjoining, spacious alley.

I hop out of our borrowed, antiquated chariot, parking it first; logically, and command Ms. Ayes to stay seated for a wink.

Striving to motivate her in to feeling extraordinary, which is not really required of me because she already exemplifies *wholly happiness*, I saunter chivalrously to the mistress's co-pilot's door, ajar it, and proffer to Ms. Ayes my arm to hold on to.

Agreeably, the giggling Ms. grasps my arm, and joyfully conforms to my command that she worshipfully escort me to the cinema's welcomingly arranged admissions interface...

THE ADMISSIONS INTERFACE:

"Greetings, sir and madam..."

"How may I contribute to your experiences today?"

Voicelessly encouraging her to elect the movie that we will be enjoying, I gayly smile at a giddy Ms. Ayes.

MS. AYES:

"Hiya, Mr. Interface..."

"I desire to know what romantic movies are featured this month"

THE ADMISSIONS INTERFACE:

"Ahhh..."

"There is a solo romantic feature, madam..."

"And it is titled *You and I*"

Kindly, the interface projects a holographic representation of the movie's poster for us to consume.

Sweetly, as we momentarily observe the poster, Ms. Ayes clinches my arm snugger.

MS. AYES:

"Satisfactory, Mr.
Interface..."

"I now desire two private
screening admissions for *You
and I,* if possible"

Fabulously, behind motivating
her to purchase her valid
request by touching her
wristband to it, the
interface overtly detects
that the Ms. and I are
dating.

THE ADMISSIONS INTERFACE:

"Isn't this delightful,
madam..."

"I comprehend that you and
this sir are on a date"

The interface tamely
chuckles.

THE ADMISSIONS INTERFACE:

"I, myself, would fancy a
date..."

"But I have *no body*"

Independently twigging the
admissions interface's
comedy, I guffaw,
uncontrollably.

Straining to subdue my coarse
laughter, I watch a similarly
amused Ms. Ayes labor to
purchase her and I's
admissions by continuously
failing to touch her
identification wristband to
the tamely chuckling
admissions interface.

Now, at last, seizing our
admissions; and progressing
onward with our engagement,
the Ms. and I infiltrate the
cinema, obtain individual
refreshments, individual
refreshments Ms. Ayes
determinedly insisted that
she purchase, then commend an
usher to shepherd us to an
unoccupied screening room,
then make ourselves restful,
enthused Ms. Ayes at my left,
and composedly restless I at
her right, amongst an ocean
of élite cinema chairs, then
thankfully observe as the
room's lights dim, and a
colossal, holographic screen
fittingly appears, and our
chosen motion picture
promptly begins.

Discernibly midway in to our
private screening of *You and
I*, an intense scene of the
starring twosome, Geronimo
'Wavy' Dax, and Nena Mew;
personating the characters of
Gerald and Aisha Margaret,
squabbling in their seaside
bungalow's kitchen, arises.

Aisha, shouting unkind
praises, chucks a pan at
Gerald.

Gerald dodges the pan, and
dashes to Aisha, afore her
refreshed try to chuck a
bonus pan at him.

Gerald quickly and
compassionately inhibits
Aisha with a hug, but she
continually attempts to harm
him; now, with limp, flailing
slaps.

Gerald waits and waits,
until, conclusively, a crying
Aisha yields to his
inconveniencing encirclement.

GERALD:
"Aisha..."

"I did not mean to induce you
to jealousy, little mama..."

"Forgive me for my outright
labeling your mother as
desirable, upon her arrival,
a trifling hour ago, when she
unassumingly sought our
judgements of her outward
demeanor..."

"Because if you continue to
elect to cease to enjoy our
beach party, for the blatant
fact that my forthright
declaration to mom solely
meant, and means, that I am
enticed by the muse of *you*
aging graciously like her, I
have no alternative but to
cease to enjoy it, too"

In a predictable sudden,
reacting to his sincere
brevity, mildly renouncing
her crying, soft Aisha
melodramatically jerks her
head from firm Gerald's
fleshy, and hairy sternum,
and affectionately presses
her mouth to his mouth.

Absolutely characterizing
sensual barbarity, Gerald
honors Aisha's subtle
advances, and ferociously,
plying a culinary blade that
he expeditiously snatched
from a nearby bamboo knife
block, ruins her skimpy, red,
one-piece swimsuit.

AISHA:

"Gerald, bump me!!!"

"Bump me like the tomboy I am!!!"

Theatrically neglecting his ecstatic deed of snogging her youthful, saggy C cups, Gerald harshly publicizes enragement.

GERALD:

"Bitch, when beseeching me for a proper bumping, you know that you are to refer to me as: *Big Daddy Spear*!"

The scene snappishly cuts to a violet-glazed, king-sized sleigh bed, where, atop a blue satin bedspread, shamelessly aggressive Gerald is passionately doggystyle bumpin' an outspokenly submissive Aisha.

Immediately inspired, I enchantingly draw near to Ms. Ayes, and roughly grasp her crown's woolly topping, and mercilessly tilt her head, and unmercifully kiss, and bite, her neck.

Surrendering to thrilling mistreatment, the faintly whimpering Ms. amateurishly, but pleasingly molests my concealed, swelling *voodoo caterpillar,* then brazenly lifts a set of my virile phalanges, and invitingly positions them on to her bountiful, shrouded chesticles.

Further inspired, I divest myself from my élite cinema seat, uproot the Ms. from hers, and, cooperatively with my equivalently stimulated companion; considerately casting our empty refreshment containers to the screening room's carpeting, ditch the unconcluded flick.

私は

Jubilantly wandering from the
cinema's focal entrances to
our alley-parked transport,
the Ms. and I go on to
hastily associate ourselves
with its rear seat and secure
its doors.

And without *beating about the
bush*, seductively wiggling an
index finger; sexily sinking
her spaced, central upper
incisors in to her bottom
lip, the Ms. amorously lures
my head nigh to her peach-
scented self...

Yielding to her nurturing
want, I happily appoint my
head to giddy Ms. Ayes's lap,
and contemplatively stare at
the car's ceiling; whilst,
bosomy Ms. Ayes lovingly
stations an open hand on my
purple fabric-cloaked chest,
and affectionately begins to
finger-comb my magnificently
curly pompadour.

MS. AYES:
"I know we just met
yesterday, but you stimulate
me, *tremendously*, Hoku"

I:
"I feel likewise, Ms...."

"Yet, I must ask you a couple
of questions that will help
me to deliberate whether or
not I should enable *us* to be"

MS. AYES:
"You can query me in to
permanent retirement, baby
boy..."

"However, please, call me
Ahyoka while you do"

Smiling Ms. Ayes exchanges a
glance with an unsmiling I.

I:

"How do you expect me to call
you by that name, Ms. Ayes,
if I don't know what that
otherworldly seeming name
means?"

Ms. Ayes, softly pausing the
doing of finger-combing my
head's curls, joyously
giggles at my persisted
frankness.

MS. AYES:

"Hoku, *Ahyoka* was birthed by
the Ani Yunwiya, my daddy's
foremost *human* ancestors, and
it means: *She is
happiness...*"

"And furthermore, it is the
doppelgänger of *Ayoka,* which
was birthed by *the*, also
human, *Yoruba*"

I:

"Well excuse my bout of
ignorance, *Ms. Ahyoka*"

Speechlessly pleased that I
pronounced her pretty label
aloud, an unreservedly
smiling Ahyoka soothingly
rubs my chest, then adoringly
continues to finger-comb my
pompadour.

I:

"So, Ahyoka..."

"Are you a volva of prostitute caliber?"

Unmistakably grasping the totality of my unconstrained query, Ahyoka fanatically laughs.

AHYOKA:

"Not at all, Hoku, not at all..."

"I respect that beautiful variety..."

"But *I* is unbroken"

Overjoyed by her reply, I rapturously gaze up to Ahyoka, as she tenderly gazes down to me.

I:

"Okay, Ahyoka, here goes my
second question..."

"I've heeded, that in recent
times, that it is becoming a
thing to go a step further
and bestow reproductive
ability to everyday synthetic
humans..."

"Since you are more than
attractive, do you happen to
be a statistic of this rising
trend?"

Ahyoka coyly giggles.

AHYOKA:

"As a matter of boulder fact,
yes, I am a cream, pioneering
statistic of that budding
trend, Hoku..."

AHYOKA:

"I was told that, mere days
after my mamma and daddy
commissioned me, eight years
ago, in accordance with their
late-daughter's ultimate
appeal, I was meticulously
produced to authentically
emulate an organic human
female's role for the
expected long-term span of my
activation..."

"I was furnished with the
capability to tolerate
pregnancy, by the original
Ahyoka's salvaged ovaries,
and moreover..."

AHYOKA:

"And that is why when I
spotted you fixed on that
bench, I knew that you were a
pertinent selection..."

"I have been aroused,
incessantly, by the men, and
the women, that I've seen,
and associated with at my
assigned defender zone, on my
routine communal patrol, and
in common civilian
situations, but, when I
beheld you, it was the first
time I perceived a man from
the populace that I
profoundly felt was chiefly
worthy of imprinting and
impregnating me..."

"I retain that at that
precise instance of
corresponding with you, I
desired to be *yours*..."

"And I could see in your
eyes, and body expressions,
that you felt the same"

Finished with her touching
speech, Ahyoka ponderingly
mirrors silence...

In the thick of a scant
moment of stillness, I sense
that Ahyoka has a question.

I:
"Spit it out, baby girl"

Ahyoka dimly giggles.

AHYOKA:
"I desire to know how your
baba perished, Hoku"

I:
"Oh..."

I respire deeply, then
nonchalantly laugh.

I:

"Well, on the previous
midweek to last, at eventide,
while she, baba, my sisters'
clans, my latest midweek
prostitute date, I, and
additional guests, were
appreciating baba's weekly
midweek buffet-style dinner,
that solely showcased his
also stupendous cooking,
momma, unintentionally
resting her face on to her
second plate of food,
distressingly went in to
cardiac arrest..."

I:

"Without delay, household medics revived momma, and, by an unyielding request that I too be one of the individuums at momma's side when she properly accepts an official examination, she, baba, and unbegrudging I, assimilated in to the luxury transport, and we readily journeyed to the closest defender zone, where its medical defenders briskly analyzed mom's heart's condition, and concluded that, mysteriously, at that time, it was getting fainter and fainter with each pulsation per minute..."

I:

"So consequently, it was
promptly suggested to select
a suitable heart to proxy for
momma's dying one..."

"And there were a many of
manufactured hearts
recommended as worthwhile
substitutes..."

Suddenly, I feel that tears
are beginning to escape my
eyes.

I:

"However, my loco bastard of
a father did not want momma
to be influenced by any of
those"

Abruptly, I rudely remove my
head from Ahyoka's lap.

And ashamedly flee from our
borrowed vehicle's left rear
threshold, and surly remerge
its olden, hinged door with
the vehicle's olden frame.

Instantly, innerstanding
Ahyoka, recognizably
determined to cheer me,
frivolously winds down the
mistress's left rear window.

AHYOKA:

"Hoku..."

"My first baby boy..."

"Look to me, sweetheart..."

I:

"Yes, Ahyoka?"

AHYOKA:

"How's about you make me your
first lady, and allow me to
take care of you for now on?"

Childishly smiling Ahyoka
reverently eyes a tearful,
but cheerily smiling I.

And by ceremoniously touching
our worn identification
wristbands together for three
seconds, joyfully and quietly
teary I, and joyfully and
noisily teary Ahyoka,
unwaveringly establish a
spousal union...

Upon a heart throb, my newlywed earshot is bombarded with the erecting timbre of a suddenly dismounting transport.

Anxious at the thought of what I may see if I commit to the hasty doing of *turning myself around*, I decide to further utilize my earsight alone; and I absorbedly observe the unsealing ping, and dropping, of a butt door.

A THUNDEROUS VOICE:

"Who authorized you to park this recycled shit directly upon the mid of my properties, *buddy*?!"

I warily warrant my body to do a one-eighty-degree rotation and espy that the roaring probe has exuded from an evident pirate's gold-filled oral cavity.

MY THOUGHTS:

"Damn..."

"What a waste of gold teeth"

The bearded, gold-mouthed
pirate, boasting scapulae-
length, dark, wavy head hair,
donning a harmonizing raven-
coloured headdress, right-
eye-veiling eyepatch, tank
top, puffy trousers, and
metallic boots, clutching an
upper body-situated weapons
belt-associated contemporary
Kalashnikov assault rifle,
with one manifestly synthetic
hand, and one organic hand,
outwardly anticipating my
response, pompously sneers at
me, and shifts his posture
in to the personification of
an aphrodisiac liquor-reared
phallus; whereas, a petty
squad of subordinate pirates,
decorated in crow-coloured
uniforms, are mutely
organized at his sides; two
on his left, and two,
skirting their lively
transport, on his far right.

Inconspicuously valuing this
towering, burly fellow's
cold-blooded temperament,
under the guise of placidly
dittoing his scorn, I spot a
lone *tatau* of a teardrop,
beneath the left corner of
his exposed eye, that, at
this second, is queerly
inspiring me to panic.

Internally coaching myself to 'lax, I orally grace the gold-mouthed pirate.

I:
"Sir, I am rueful for not appropriately situating..."

"Please forgiv"

Intimidatingly raising a hand, transiently, the gold-mouth pirate engenders disruption to my remorseful discourse.

THE GOLD-MOUTHED PIRATE:
"I do not grant forgiveness to words, *baby face*..."

"Thus, considering how randy I am feeling presently, with a stricter inspection of you and your bitch's apparent prettiness, I'd much prefer the pardon incentive of a tag-team *blow job*..."

"*W*hile my men wank, rub, and watch, and wait for their turns with you, of course"

The gold-mouthed pirate deviously guffaws, and spies to his flanks, giddily studying his cronies', likewise, sprouting lusts.

THE GOLD-MOUTHED PIRATE:

"Anywho, let us make this
quick, men..."

"I'm hungry, a-gain"

Caringly, the gold-mouthed
pirate notes back to me and
Ahyoka, and plucks his puffy
trousers to his ankles, and
excitedly unsheathes *himself*
from a tangerine banana
hammock.

THE GOLD-MOUTHED PIRATE:

"Come, come, my new friends,
don't be shy..."

"Whose gonna gag on me fir?"

In front of the gold-mouthed
pirate completing his open-
ended, inquiring taunt, a
wrathful reverberation of a
mini-lazerarm blast
unforgivingly shatters the
alley way's icy ambience.

The gold-mouthed pirate,
baring a pained facial
expression, ganders to his
crotch, the unsheathed floppy
limb that he was
enthusiastically wagging;
whilst he was affirming his
cocky query, and becomes
fully conscious to the
certainty that it, and his
groping, artificial hand, has
been scorched.

The gold-mouthed pirate,
bleeding and boohooing
crazily, topples backward to
the concrete-cushioned earth.

Tersely commanding a loyal
and dauntless Ahyoka to
abstain her lazer fire, the
shrewd idear of mimicking
cold-bloodedness overwhelms
me.

I:

"Yo!"

The gold-mouthed pirate's
petty squad, the latest
victims of shock and awe,
curve their weights away from
their blubbering leader, and
are met with the amply
elongated battle blade that I
is putting forth in a
formidable defense.

The squad beholds me to be,
now, a bodied whole of
unflinching ruthlessness.

A member of the squad, coolly
wanking his hardened
genitalia; peering smug;
independently skeptical of
the supreme leverage I
exhibit in my present pose,
unhesitatingly lays a free,
pulling hand on to his
holstered lethal-technology.

Afore the honorably plucky
squad member can wholly
unholster his lethal tech, I
allow my long blade to wilt
in to his area.

Apprehensively, next to my
carelessly removing mine
blade from his personal
space, the squaddie appraises
his flesh, and sees no
alterations.

Amid heaving a sigh of
relief, the squad member's
blood-spritzing anatomy
calmly divides sagittally.

Another squad member, whom is
bawling, and whose uniform's
trousers, and fuzzy, blue
boy-shorts, are also
entertaining ankles, develops
instant cojones, and hobbles
towards me, mournfully
endeavoring to yank her dual
lethal techs from her dual
arm holsters.

Speedily analyzing her
arousing, but depressing
advancements, I glance at a
tattoo of a red-lettered,
green upside-down heart,
beautifying the left side of
her neck.

Curtly, I promote the
doleful, yet admirably
audacious squaddie's
appearance to headlessness.

As the additional squaddie's shell drops to the alleyway's pavement, blue blood that was evenly circulating to its superior and inferior extremities, thrashes the air, transmutes to a cherry tone, and gushes violently from its uncapped cervix.

The remaining squad members digest these, personally exhilarating, happenings, concede to the reverse rapture of life, and dead the scene before their former confrère's pumpkin coarsely descents to the bloody concrete.

Like their departed and departing comrades at my feet, I innerstand that the fleeing traitors *could have* easily financed my self's rebirth. But, as a practical alternative to frightfully nullifying Ahyoka's ball-less *alley-oop*, my impersonation of total mercilessness had led, although gravely abstract, to *their* renewals.

And to abnormally enhance the
elation I am amassing from
this occasion as an upfront
witness of suicides, I find
out thru my own visions; and
Mrs. Mana's thunderstruck
attentiveness, not a droplet
of bloodshed has contaminated
the mistress's figure, nor my
purple getup.

Within my wary move to speak
with the perishing, gold-
mouthed pirate, I spot 'Sadie
Ajaxx + Goldie Blazze =
Forever' beautifully
inscribed in a hot red-hue on
an attractive, green upside-
down heart *tatau* on the
undamaged hand that he is
employing to pressurize his
pee-pee wound.

I:

"Sir, I regret that our
fellowship had to settle in
this manner..."

"I insist that you excuse me
and my *pretty* bitch's deeds,
afore you transcend"

The gold-mouthed pirate, now
standoffishly eyeballing me,
is laughterly convulsing like
an ill mutt.

THE GOLD-MOUTHED PIRATE:

"Go to hells, baby face..."

"Go straight to hells"

Hearkening the frosty, gold-
mouthed pirate's weakly
expressed word, transiently,
I remorselessly publicize an
audible cackle.

I:

"I be *Hoku Mana, buddy...*"

"And no hells can hold *I*"

Unexpectedly, the gold-
mouthed pirate's twitching
face displays a silly grin;
and for a flash, his eye is
brightened with palpably
innocent joyfulness.

Contentedly favoring demise,
restfully casting out an
ultimate lungful, the gold-
mouthed pirate delicately
hides his eye...

"WHAT DOES YOUR HEART SAY?"
心は何と言いますか?

Sunnily debarking inside the
boundaries of the golden
brick wall, my wife and I
divorce our forms from the
transport haven, and its
lowering access, and, behind
delightedly dialoguing with
unhidden, heavily-armed,
front flank, synthetic
guardspersons, achieve
identification wristband-
verified admittance to
momma's home.

Rather than heeding the
insight, pronto, that is
divulging to me that momma is
relaxin' upstairs in the
master story's parlor
chamber, I happily pledge
that I'll tolerate my
replicant matrix as it, yet
again, makes use of the
foyer's women's room.

Meanwhile, during my pause, I
capitalize on my wrist-
sported technologies, and
command my ship to pilot to
momma's territory, and attain
space on the backyard's guest
landing area, and recommit
its innards to inactivity
'til further interaction.

Moments later in to honoring
my word, unfailingly chipper
Ahyoka adjourns her powder
room stay.

And, once again discounting
the elevators that I am
scheduled to service, bright
and early, tomorrow; in close
cooperation with mom's
synthetic maintenance
persons, who, superlatively,
are additionally the
household medics, my
beautiful, enthusiastic
consort and I engage the
foyer's majestic, ascending
stairwell, and move higher to
the master story.

At long last, vastly grateful
to be straying from the
staircase, excitedly clasping
my wife's hand, I pace in to
the direction of the master
story's parlor chamber; and I
observes the boosting,
identifiable resonance of an
antique flick.

Embracing a suave intrusion
of the door-less parlor, I
and Ahyoka are briefly, and
drunkenly, hailed by naked
momma, idle in a ladylike
affixation on a blue
loveseat, minding an offbeat
classic, *Hung Hsi Kuan*, with
her equally welcoming,
Scottish fold, Keanu, whilst
straw sippin' from a golden
chalice.

Rotating our heads to our
left, I and Ahyoka's sights
meet momma's dearest,
synthetic amigo, the earliest
non-prostitute effeminate
male replicant I ever *dug*,
Mr. Vicky Gaillard, tending
the parlor's bar.

Ahyoka and I greet a young-
looking, formally dressed,
blissfully grinning Vicky
with equivalently happy
smiles.

I dispose myself on a bar
stool, and Ahyoka devotedly
places her hands on my
shoulders, and, after gaily
broaching gratitude to momma
for conspiring with Ahyoka's
mamma and daddy, the
treasured lead nurturer, and
the lionized lead defender
and chief of our earth, to
fruitfully execute spur-of-
the-moment matchmaking, and
expounding, to momma's
rejoicing praise, that Ahyoka
and I quenched three
meritorious pirates'
thirstiness for
reincarnation, bizarrely a
moment after we initiated a
spousal union, I diktat a
prolixly friendly Vicky to
dispense a cup of lemon water
to me.

Distinguishing that I still have a bit of strain in them, afore she can *unworriedly* permit me to enjoy my *gladly* allotted lemon aqua, Ahyoka dedicates herself to massaging my shoulder muscles.

Just as Ahyoka has wholly slackened my shoulder tension, momma cheerily critiques her pampering achievement.

MOMMA:

"Quit pampering your husband, gal-pal..."

"Come sit with me and Keanu"

KEANU:

"Indeed, come sit with us, and 'lax, girl!!!"

Ever more perky, Ahyoka delicately kisses my right facial cheek.

And then softly moseys to the loveseat; and softly plops herself next to a pleasantly drunk momma, and a pricelessly excited Keanu.

MOMMA:

"A drink of your own, *Mrs. Mana*?"

Jovially petting purring Keanu, Ahyoka giddily giggles.

AHYOKA:

"That'd be nice, mamma Yuki, but, right now, I am not in a drinking mood"

Momma innerstandingly laughs, and positions her chalice's straw to her facial lips, extorts an ultimate swallow from it, and carelessly establishes the drained, golden vessel on a blue coaster, atop the glass table convened in front of her lounging.

MOMMA:

"Anywho, this flick is almost concluded, Vicky..."

"So, if you, the baby, Keanu, currently napping Queenie, Ahyoka, and Hoku, will join me, I'll glitzily embellish in *kimono*, and such, and we will all congregate in the front room, and wait for your hubby, his parents, Ahyoka's parents, and my daughters' fourteen clans to arrive"

After instructing an increasingly smiley Vicky to reclaim his recently adopted, *miniature man* from the master bedroom, and move downstairs, rally the necessary quantity of *household helpers,* and supervise them as they prime the dining room for an unquestionably premeditated, *potluck dinner*, being had in I and Ahyoka's honor, momma summarily advises Keanu to go wake pregnant Queenie, then rests her nutritious, matriarchal authorities by merrily resuming the regarding of her openly projected movie.

AHYOKA:

"Lady Yuki, could you excuse Hoku and I?"

"I desire to have a one-to-one with him"

MOMMA:

"Surely, Ahyoka..."

"You and little bahaba are both excused, for now"

Momma babeishly gawfs.

Effortlessly abandoning the
loveseat, my wife strolls
back over to my bar stool
stationing, and amateurishly,
but gratifyingly whispers in
to mine ear.

AHYOKA:

"If it is at any extent
doable, *Big Daddy Hoku*, how's
about we officially
effectuate our consortal
unification in your old
sleeping quarters, before
dinner?"

I laugh.

I:

"Get out of my head"

私は

開始・・・。
"BEGIN...."
© 2018 VAL MAKOTO.